For Sasha and Rose
R. L.

For Eric
J. M.

First edition 2004

Library of Congress Cataloging-in-Publication Data

Lindbergh, Reeve.
Our nest / Reeve Lindbergh ; illustrated by Jill McElmurry. —1st ed.
p. cm.
Summary: A rhymed view of the interrelatedness and belonging
of all things and creatures in the universe, from the stars,
to the sea, to a mouse, to a child.
ISBN 0-7636-1286-3
[1. Universe—Fiction. 2. Stories in rhyme.]
I. McElmurry, Jill, ill. II. Title
PZ8.3.L6148 Ou 2003
[E]—dc21   2001058197

2 4 6 8 10 9 7 5 3 1

Printed in China

This book was typeset in Godlike.
The illustrations were done in gouache.

Candlewick Press
2067 Massachusetts Avenue
Cambridge, Massachusetts 02140

visit us at www.candlewick.com

Our Nest

REEVE LINDBERGH

illustrated by JILL McELMURRY

CANDLEWICK PRESS
CAMBRIDGE, MASSACHUSETTS

Snuggled in bed,
You're all safe and warm,
Like a bird in a nest in a tree.

The dog curls up
At your feet with a sigh,
And sleeps with his head
On your knee.

Our cat made a nest in a pile of clothes,
Her kittens were born there one day.

A hen made a nest in the loft of our barn
And laid speckled eggs in the hay.

A mouse has a nest in an old garden glove

That was left at the edge of the lawn.

There's a nest of low grass

In the field by the wall

Where a doe spends the night

With her fawn.

In back of the wall is a brush pile,
Filled with brambles and branches of trees,
And a chipmunk who rests
In his thick-tangled nest,
In a dark place that nobody sees.

In the marsh we have red-winging blackbirds who sing
From the tops of the cattails and reeds,
And a quiet brown duck keeps her ducklings all safe
In a nest tucked away in the weeds.

A little brook runs from the marsh through the farm.
It winds and re-winds, in and out,
And the willowy shade that these windings have made
Leaves a watery nest for the trout.

The brook winds on farther and farther,
Flowing into the river at last,
Where a nest of green valleys enfolds it,
And the river runs on, wide and fast.

The river goes down through the valley,
And then through the town to the shore,
Where big boats that roam on the ocean come home
To the nest of the harbor once more.

The earth makes a nest for the ocean,
And holds the wet world of the sea,
Where the fish and the whales
And the wind-driven sails
Are all rocked by the waves, wild and free.

The universe carries the earth and the moon
And the planets, like Venus and Mars.
The vastness of space, that mysterious place,
Is a nest for the sun and the stars.

All things together are in the same nest—

The sun and the moon and the sea,

The boats and the harbor,
The brook and the river,

The doe and the mouse,
You and me.

We're here in the nest of creation
With the earth and the stars up above.

And you're here, safe and warm,
In the nest of my arms,
When I wrap them around you with love.